教育部国别与区域研究之江西理工大学巴基斯坦研究中心招标课题阶段性成果

中国经典美德故事

Chinese Classic Virtue Stories

李火秀　邓 琳◎编著

ZHEJIANG UNIVERSITY PRESS

浙江大学出版社

总　序

海外华文教育主要是针对海外华人进行的中国语言文化教育。 伴随着我国经济的快速发展、全球化进程的加快和"一带一路"倡议的提出，世界各地的华文教育，正以前所未有的速度向前推进。 当前，华文教育的内容、范畴、功能、目标都从单一走向多元，华文教育教学不仅注重汉语的语音、词汇、语法、汉字等中文基础知识的讲解，而且还以弘扬中华文化、塑造中国形象、提升华人的民族文化素质与文化认同感，促进中外文化交流，增进中外友谊为重要目标。 中华文化及相关内涵精神的独特魅力，通过华文教育教学，获得了海外华人以及越来越多非华裔外国人的了解、熟悉和应用，中华文化及其所蕴含的普适性价值在异域大放光彩。 基于此，海外同胞把华文教育视作"留根工程"，同时也是提高后代素质，参与竞争的"希望工程"，其意义重大而深远。

在这一新形势下，我校（江西理工大学）始终坚持开放办学的思想，在教育国际化和华文教育工作方面取得了可喜成绩。截至目前，我校与美国、英国、法国、韩国、日本、泰国等 20 多个国家的高校和企业建立了交流与合作关系。其中，与泰国宋卡王子大学的合作交流，早在 20 多年前就已经展开，双方每年都开展多次师生互访并联合培养博士、硕士研究生。近年来，面对国内外华文教育迅猛发展的形势，我校于 2008 年创办对外汉语专业（后更名为汉语国际教育专业）；2011 年 11 月，国务院侨务办公室下发《关于同意江西理工大学建立华文教育基地的批复》的文件，使我校成为江西第二个、赣州第一个华文教育基地；2012 年 3 月，我校外语外贸学院成立了"江西理工大学华文教育研究中心"；2014 年 12 月，学校同意将研究中心升级为校级科研平台进行管理和建设；2015 年我校与巴基斯坦旁遮普大学签署共建孔子学院的协议，实现了我校在海外设立孔子学院的重大历史性突破。2017 年 6 月，教育部下发了《关于公布 2017 年

教育部国别和区域研究中心备案名单的通知》，我校申报的巴基斯坦研究中心成功获批备案。 所有这些喜人的成绩离不开我校各级领导在华文教育教学和管理工作方面的夙夜在公、殚精竭虑，离不开所有教师的恪尽职守、勤勉敬业，离不开所有与华文教育教学工作相关教师的勠力同心、砥砺奋进。 当然，我们深知中华传统文化博大精深，要将我国传统文化发扬光大，使传统文化在当代引起共鸣与认同，我们责无旁贷，任重而道远。

为此，我们编写了一套"魅力汉语·悦读经典"丛书，精选中华传统文化，文学中最经典、最有价值的神话传说、寓言故事、美德故事、戏剧故事等。 本套丛书为了便于读者能够独立阅读，在保持原著精髓的基础上，采用平实流畅、简洁生动的语言讲述故事。 每篇故事均配汉语拼音、中英文对照、故事寓意的品读，并且每篇都绘制了一幅精美插图。另外，丛书对一些生难字词做了中英文注释。 这些都可以让读者增强阅读印象，更好地领略经典名作的魅力，体验人类

最高尚的情感和最珍贵的品质，进而提升知识理解水平和审美鉴赏能力，获得心灵的滋养和精神的洗礼。

　　本套丛书不仅可以成为汉语学习者学习汉语、理解中华文化的专门读本，也可以成为英语学习者扩大阅读视野、提升英语水平的专门文本。当然，丛书中精选的内容同样可以成为广大文学爱好者品读经典，了解中国传统文化的通识读物。

Foreword

Chinese language and culture education, mainly aiming at teaching the overseas Chinese language and culture of China, is advancing at an unprecedented speed, along with the rapid economic development, accelerated globalization and proposing of the Belt and Road Initiative. Currently, the content, category, function and goal of Chinese language and culture education have developed from simplification to diversification. It not only focuses on imparting Chinese phonetics, vocabulary, grammar, and Chinese characters, but also aims to advance the Chinese culture, shape China's image in the world, improve the overseas Chinese people's national cultural awareness and identity, promote the Sino-foreign cultural exchange and strengthen the Sino-foreign friendship. Chinese culture and the charm of its connotations are understood, well-known and used by more and more overseas Chinese and non-Chinese foreigners through the Chinese language and culture education. The universal values of Chinese culture are shining brightly overseas. Besides, overseas Chinese regard the Chinese language and culture education as the "Root

Project" and the "Hope Project" which aims at improving the descendants'
cultural accomplishment, carrying great and profound significance.

In this new situation, Jiangxi University of Science and Technology
insists on the running of open education and has made great achievements on
international education as well as the Chinese language and culture education.
Till now, our university has set up collaborative relationships with universities
and enterprises in more than 20 countries like the USA, the UK, France, R. O.
Korea, Japan, Thailand, etc. The collaboration with Prince of Songkla
University started over twenty years ago. Each year, many teachers and
students pay exchange visits between our university and Prince of Songkla
University where doctoral candidates and postgraduates have been co-
cultivated. In recent years, as Chinese language and culture education has
rapidly developed, our university began to recruit students majoring in Teaching
Chinese as a Foreign Language in 2008 which was later renamed as Chinese
International Education. In November, 2011, the Overseas Chinese Affairs
Office issued the file "Approval of Jiangxi University of Science and
Technology as the Chinese Language and Cultural Education Base" which enabled

us to be the second Chinese language and culture education base in Jiangxi Province and the first one in Ganzhou City. In March, 2012, a research center of Chinese language and culture education was set up in our faculty and then upgraded as a university research platform in December, 2014. Next year, a Confucius Institute was co-founded overseas by Pakistan's Punjab University and us, which was a historic breakthrough. The Pakistan Research Center in our university was in the name list reported for record as the National and Regional Research Centers approved by the Ministry of Education of China in June, 2017. All these achievements are attributed to the hard work of leaders and teachers at all levels in our university and particularly those teachers working for the Chinese language and culture education. Of course, we surely know the extensiveness and profoundness of traditional Chinese culture. Therefore, we will spare no effort to promote and develop traditional Chinese culture to gain more acceptance and resonance in the contemporary world.

For this purpose, we compiled this series named "Charming Chinese, Classic Reading", in which the most classic, valuable stories in the form of

myths, fables, virtue and drama stories about traditional Chinese culture and literature were selected. To enable readers to do the reading pleasantly, all the stories in both Chinese and English, with a vivid picture at the beginning and comment at the end, are edited with plain, concise but vivid words, going with Chinese characters and corresponding pinyin. Besides, notes are given for some difficult words. In this way, readers may have a joyful reading experience to appreciate the charm of the classics, the noblest emotions and the precious characters of humans, which in turn will help them improve their comprehension and aesthetic appreciation ability and eventually receive spiritual nourishment and baptism.

This series of stories render learners of Chinese a way to learn Chinese language and culture, broaden their reading vision and improve their English reading ability. Meanwhile, these books can be a good choice for those lovers of literature to learn traditional Chinese culture.

前　言

中华传统美德是中华民族几千年历史、文化绵延不息、凝练而成的社会道德准则，是中华民族传统文化的灵魂，展现了中华民族优良的道德品质、崇高的民族气节和高尚的民族情感。中华传统美德涵盖的内容博大精深，历经千年的流传、发展，已经具有比较稳固、确切的意义内涵：仁、义、礼、智、信。

（1）"仁"，是指"仁爱之心"，对他人秉持友爱、关心、同情和理解的态度。孔子认为"仁"是道德品格的最高境界，他说，"志士仁人，无求生以害仁，有杀身以成仁"，意思是不惜牺牲自己的生命来维护"仁"。可见，"仁"在中华传统美德中占有极为重要的地位。

（2）"义"，是指担当、正直、无私和道义。《说文解字》中这样解释："义，己之威仪也。从我羊。"即用羊的温驯、和善来形容人的仪表和涵养，要像羊一样温和、善良、美好。孟子十分推崇"义"，他说要"舍生取义"。

这与孔子"杀身以成仁"的说法是一致的。 人们通常会说"仁义道德",表明"仁"和"义",是中华传统美德中两大核心要素。

（3）"礼",是指礼貌、礼仪和礼节。"礼"最初是原始社会用来祭祀祈福的一种习俗和仪式。 后来,随着社会的发展,"礼"成为规范人的言行举止的道德准则,它倡导人们要在合适妥当、恰如其分的道德规范中立身、处世。 中国人向来十分注重礼仪规范,使自己的一言一行、一举一动都能够符合"礼"的规定。 由此可见,"礼"在中华传统美德中同样有着非常重要的地位。

（4）"智",是指智慧、聪明,能够辨别是非、善恶的一种能力和德行。 孔子在《论语》中说,"知之为知之,不知为不知,是知也",意思是要有实事求是的态度,知道就是知道,不知道就是不知道,这样才是真正的智慧。 表明"智"不仅是聪颖、智慧的表征,而且"智"教育人们要具有

真诚、坦诚的价值取向。因而，"智"作为一种基本的思想道德和文明素质，成为传统美德中重要的一维。

（5）"信"，是指信用、信誉和信义。它要求人们要诚实守信、坚定可靠。程颐说，"人无忠信，不可立于世"，意思是说人如果不讲忠诚信用，就不能够在社会上立足。因而，"信"不仅倡导人们自身做到诚实可靠，而且也提倡人与人之间做到相互信赖，讲求信誉。中华民族历来尊崇"信"的道德品质，把诚信看作为人处世的基本道德规范。

"仁、义、礼、智、信"的关系密切，相互依存，共同构筑成为中华民族传统道德规范的核心。围绕这一核心，它不断地延展出诸多相近或相同的表述，如精忠报国、勤政爱民、修身律己、刚正不阿、爱岗敬业、谦恭有礼、尊老爱幼、尊师重教、团结友爱、勤奋刻苦等美好的道德品质。这些传统美德对个人修身养性、家庭伦理乃至治国安邦都具有举足轻重的作用，对社会发展、文明进步产生了广泛且深远的影响。

　　《中国经典美德故事》精心择取我国历史上一些著名人物具有代表性的美德故事，将其分为精忠爱国、孝悌好礼、诚实守信、勤奋好学四大类，共计 32 则故事并对其进行编排。 本书采用故事加注拼音与中英文对照、生难字词中英文注释的方式，以精练的语言讲述故事。 每篇都有精彩的故事品读，并根据情节配以精美的插图。 每一辑后面收录十则名人名言，让读者更为深入地了解那些代代相传、历久弥新的名章典故、名言警句。

　　品读美德经典，构筑精彩人生，让生命在阅读中得到升华，让人生在阅读中更加充实。

编　者

2017 年 12 月 15 日

Preface

Traditional Chinese virtue is the moral ethics of the Chinese nation shaped and polished throughout thousands of years, by the Chinese culture and history. It is the soul of Chinese nation's traditional culture, showing the excellent moral character, sublime national integrity and lofty national emotion. With profound and extensive contents, its connotation has been defined uniformly as benevolence, righteousness, etiquette, wisdom and faithfulness.

(1) Benevolence refers to the kind attitude towards others with fraternal love, care, sympathy and understanding. It is regarded as the highest moral standard that may be protected and defended by one's life, as can be seen in Confucius' saying: "A man of lofty ideals and benevolence should not, at the expense of benevolence, cling cravenly to life but conduct braving death. He will, on the contrary, lay down his life for the accomplishment of benevolence." Therefore, benevolence is rendered a significant position in traditional Chinese virtue.

(2) Righteousness denotes the manner of carrying responsibility, integrity, selflessness, morality and justice, as explained in *Shuo Wen Jie Zi*: "Men's righteousness can be revealed in the appearance and manner which can be learnt from sheep." The saying by using the metaphor of sheep's tameness and

kindness indoctrinates that men should be tame, kind and noble just like sheep does. Mencius spoke highly of righteousness, which can be found in his belief "give up one's life for righteousness". It goes accordingly with Confucius' claim "lay down one's life for the accomplishment of benevolence". People always advocate benevolence, righteousness and virtue, which benevolence and righteousness are the two cores of traditional Chinese virtue.

(3) Etiquette means politeness, rite and courtesy. Originally as one kind of sacrificial custom and ceremony in the primitive society, it grew into a moral ethic for correcting men's behaviors and manners. It advocates men should behave themselves within the boundary of moral ethic. Chinese people always put emphasis on rite and courtesy to follow the etiquette norm which also plays an important role in traditional Chinese virtue.

(4) Wisdom is the ability and virtue of distinguishing the right from the wrong, the good from the evil. In *The Analects of Confucius*, the saying "It is wise to hold what you know and admit what you don't know" delivers the practical and realistic attitude to be wise enough on the known and unknown things. Wisdom is not only confined to being clever or wise, but also

means possessing the value orientation of sincerity. As one basic ideology morality and civilization quality, wisdom has become an essential part of traditional Chinese virtue.

(5) Faithfulness contains the meaning of integrity, reputation and faith. It requires people to be honest and reliable. Chen Yi (1033—1107) once said, "A man without credibility cannot keep a foothold in the world." Faithfulness advocates men to be trustworthy and faithful to each other. Chinese nation has always valued faithfulness as a basic ethic that should be firmly abided by.

Being closely related and mutually dependent, the five virtues (benevolence, righteousness, etiquette, wisdom and faithfulness) build the core part of traditional Chinese ethic together, from which, many correlative expressions have arisen, like repaying motherland with supreme loyalty and patriotism, be diligent in politics and concerned about people, behaving oneself with self-restraint, not yielding to pressure with strong integrity, be passionate in one's job, be humble and polite, respecting the old and loving the young, respecting teacher and valuing education, cherishing solidarity and fraternity, be diligent and industrious, etc.

These traditional virtues not only play a decisive role in self-cultivation, family ethics and country governance but also exert extensive and profound influence on social development and civilization progress.

In *Chinese Classic Virtue Stories*, 32 representative virtue stories of famous people in history are chosen, falling into four categories of "Loyalty and Patriotism", "Filial Piety and Etiquette", "Honesty and Trustworthiness", and "Diligence and Studiousness". Stories in English are combined with corresponding Chinese and pinyin. Also included are the notes of difficult words both in English and Chinese. All these stories are told in a concise way, with refined words and wonderful comments, accompanied by beautiful illustrations. Each category is ended with ten quotations so as to help readers understand deeply the renewed stories and quotations descended from older generations.

Let us read classic virtue stories and build our splendid life. Reading makes our life sublime and colorful.

Compliers

December 15, 2017

目 录
Contents

第一辑
Part 1
精忠爱国
Loyalty and
Patriotism

i

第二辑
Part 2
孝悌好礼
Filial Piety and
Etiquette

第三辑
Part 3
诚实守信
Honesty and
Trustworthiness

中

国

经

典

美

德

故

事

第一辑　精忠爱国

Part 1　Loyalty and Patriotism

屈原投江殉国

Patriotic Qu Yuan Being a Martyr to His State

qū yuán shì zhàn guó hòu qī chǔ guó de zhèng zhì jiā wěi dà de ài guó
屈原是战国后期楚国的政治家、伟大的爱国

shī rén jù chuán qū yuán cóng xiǎo jiù cōng yǐng guò rén qín fèn hào xué
诗人。据传，屈原从小就聪颖过人，勤奋好学，

huái yǒu yuǎn dà de zhèng zhì bào fù kě wàng néng wèi guó jiā xiào lì
怀有远大的政治抱负，渴望能为国家效力。

chǔ huái wáng jí wèi hòu shí fēn xīn shǎng qū yuán de cái xué yú shì
楚怀王即位后，十分欣赏屈原的才学，于是

jiāng qū yuán zhào rù gōng zhōng yǐ fǔ zuǒ tā guǎn lǐ chǔ guó de zhèng
将屈原召入宫中，以辅佐他管理楚国的政

wù nà shí měi cì huái wáng yǔ qū yuán shāng yì guó jiā dà shì qū yuán
务。那时，每次怀王与屈原商议国家大事，屈原

都能提出独到的见解，因此深得怀王信任。可是，屈原的显赫地位也招来了奸臣的妒忌。那些奸臣在怀王面前造谣中伤屈原，说屈原居功自傲，就连皇上，他也不放在眼里。怀王听后，十分生气，就疏远和冷落了屈原，这也导致屈原的一些政治主张得不到施展。皇帝昏庸，奸臣当道，楚国国势渐渐衰弱下来。当时，相邻的秦国势力日渐增大，为了国家安危，屈原曾经多次规劝楚怀王联合齐国共同抵抗强大的秦国。可是，楚怀王却听信奸臣的话，根本不听从屈原的建议。后来楚怀王被秦昭王骗到秦国，扣押在咸阳，至死也未曾回到楚国。

楚怀王死后，顷襄王继位。顷襄王与怀王一样昏庸、自负。屈原不断地向顷襄王进谏，希望他能远离小人，励精图治，使国家强盛。然而，奸佞小人又极力地在顷襄王面前说屈原的各种坏话。顷襄王一怒之下，就把屈原流放到楚国的南疆。那时的南疆荒芜寂寥，人烟稀少，很多地方都是林原草莽。屈原在那里过着贫病交加的生活。

公元前278年，秦国攻打楚国，不费吹灰之力就攻下楚国的国都。屈原听到这个消息时，伤心得痛哭不已。这时，他已经是六十二岁的老人了。经历了十几年的流放生活，屈原从一个精力旺盛的中年汉子变成了一个饱经风霜、伤病缠身的花甲老人。他知道楚国即将灭亡了，人民将在战乱中流离失所。这一情景，对于屈原来说，无疑是最沉重的打击。他决定和楚国共存亡。就在五月初五那一天，屈原抱着一块大石头，跳到汨罗江里，以身殉国了。

Qu Yuan, a great statesman and patriotic poet of the state of Chu in the late Warring States period, was talented, diligent and studious at his early age, having great political ambition and expectation to serve his motherland.

After King Huai of Chu acceded to the throne, he appreciated Qu Yuan and appointed him to help manage the state affairs. Being trusted by the king as he could put forward original ideas whenever he discussed the state affairs with the king incurred the envy and slander from some corrupt and jealous court officials. They slandered him in front of the king, saying he was arrogant and even scorned the king who then became estranged from Qu Yuan. His political assertions were no longer accepted. The incompetent king and those treacherous court officials weakened the power of the state gradually, while the neighboring state of Qin grew stronger and stronger. Qu Yuan advocated many times to ally with Qi to resist Qin for the stability and safety of his motherland. But the fatuous king only trusted those treacherous court officials, which resulted in the king's fate of being deceived by King Zhao of Qin and detained in Xianyang forever.

King Qingxiang of Chu, another fatuous and conceited ruler, acceded to the throne. Qu Yuan suggested to the king that he should stay away from corrupt officials to strive for a prosperous and sovereign state. But slanders from Qu Yuan's peer ministers infuriated the king, and Qu Yuan was exiled to the southern frontier of Chu, a wilderness, where he led a hard and miserable life.

In 278 B. C., Qin stormed Chu and seized its capital city, without the slightest effort. Upon hearing the news, Qu Yuan, a weak and sick sixty-two-year-old man and no longer a vigorous young man after a decade of exile, cried bitterly because he saw the collapse of his motherland and the suffering of those destitute and homeless people. On the Lunar May 5, with all his bitterness, Qu Yuan drowned himself with a big stone into the Miluo River.

生难字/词注解 | Notes

政治家： 掌握着权力并对历史发展起影响的领导人物。

Statesman： A skilled, experienced, and respected political leader or figure who has exerted great influence in history.

楚国的南疆： 现在的湖北省南部和湖南省北部。

The southern frontier of Chu： The southern part of Hubei Province and the northern part of Hunan Province.

故事评点 | Story Comment

屈原一生坚持自己的理想和主张，他不愿意逢迎世俗、屈就奸佞小人。屈原的爱国精神和淡泊名利的高尚情操为后人所敬重。传说当地百姓听说屈原投江后，曾驾着小船打捞屈原的尸体，并投下粽子喂鱼，防止屈原的遗体被鱼所吞食。后来，人们把每年农历五月初五屈原殉国的那一天，定为端午节。人们用吃粽子、划龙舟的方式纪念这位伟大的爱国诗人。

Qu Yuan's unswerving spirit for his ideals and standpoint shone through his entire life. He never surrendered to vicious power or those treacherous and corrupt court officials. He is respected and admired for his patriotic spirits and noble character of being indifferent to fame and wealth. According to Chinese legend, the local people, hearing Qu Yuan had drown, rowed their boats to search for his body and threw Zongzi to feed fish, protecting his body from being bit by fish. Later, the Lunar May 5, the day when Qu Yuan died for his motherland, was named as Dragon Boat Festival on which people eat Zongzi and row dragon boats in memory of the great patriotic poet Qu Yuan.

魏征犯颜直谏

Wei Zheng Admonishing the Emperor Taizong of Tang
Regardless of His Face

táng tài zōng dāng zhèng shí qī　yǒu yí wèi míng jiào wèi zhēng de dà
唐太宗当政时期，有一位名叫魏征的大

chén　 tā cái shí chāo qún　xìng qíng gěng zhí　fán shì tā rèn wéi zhèng què de
臣。他才识超群、性情耿直，凡是他认为正确的

yì jiàn　bì dìng háo bù liú qíng de dāng miàn zhí jiàn　 wèi zhēng de jìn jiàn
意见，必定毫不留情地当面直谏。魏征的进谏，

dà dào jūn guó dà shì　xiǎo dào yǐn shí qǐ jū　shàng dào huáng qīn guó qī
大到军国大事，小到饮食起居；上到皇亲国戚，

xià dào wén wǔ bǎi guān　zhǐ yào shì zài tā kàn lái bù hé lǐ de zuò fǎ　tā
下到文武百官，只要是在他看来不合理的做法，他

dōu huì háo bù liú qíng de tí chū pī píng
都会毫不留情地提出批评。

yǒu yì nián　táng tài zōng pài rén zhēng bīng　yǒu gè dà chén tí yì
有一年，唐太宗派人征兵。有个大臣提议：

未满18岁的男子，只要身材高大，就可以征招入伍。唐太宗同意了。但是魏征却扣住诏书不发。唐太宗催了几次，魏征还是不发。唐太宗忍无可忍，大发雷霆。谁知魏征却不慌不忙地说："我听说过这样一个故事。在很遥远的地方，有一个村落的人们捉鱼时喜欢让湖水流干了。这样虽能够得到鱼，但是到明年湖中就没有鱼可捞了；把树林烧光捉野兽，也会捉到野兽，但是到明年就没有野兽可捉了。如果把那些身强力壮，不到18岁的男子都征来当兵，以后还从哪里征兵呢？国家的租税杂役，又由谁来负担呢？"唐太宗听了，很是赞同。于是，又重新下了一道诏书，免征不到18岁的男子。

在皇帝的个人享乐生活方面，魏征也时常提出建议。一次，唐太宗出访洛阳，因为当地安排的饮食不合口味，太宗十分生气。魏征看见了，就当面批评太宗说："隋炀帝就是因为过度追求享乐而导致国家灭亡的。现在皇上仅仅是因为饮食招待不好就发脾气，那朝中大臣还有几个会用心为政，清正廉洁啊？人的欲望是无穷尽的，这样下去，必定会惹来祸患啊！"唐太宗听后不觉一惊，说："若不是你，我就听不到这样中肯的话了。"从那以后，太宗的生活一直十分节俭。

在和唐太宗相处的十七年里，魏征多次直言进谏。太宗想，作为一国的君主，虽然魏征的批评会让他丢了脸面，但是，魏征确实是个忠臣。所以，太宗对魏征始终怀着宽容、大度与欣赏的态度。正因为唐太宗善于听取大臣的忠告，并及时改正自己错误的决定和做法，所以才出现了历史上"贞观之治"的繁荣景象。

贞观十七年，魏征不幸病死。魏征去世后，唐太宗极为思念他，对大臣们说："用铜作镜子，可以照见衣帽是不是穿戴得端正；用历史作镜子，可以看到国家兴亡的原因；用人作镜子，可以发现自己做得对不对。我经常保留这三面镜子，防止自己犯错误。现在魏征逝世了，我就少了一面镜子啊！"

During the reign of Emperor Taizong of Tang, there was a minister named Wei Zheng who was talented and upright. From the state affairs to the meals and accommodation, he would admonish the emperor directly for what he thought to be wrong. Whatever unreasonable would be criticized by him relentlessly no matter who did it, be the royalty or the officials.

One year, Emperor Taizong of Tang made an order of conscription, while one minister advocated that conscription can be extended to the men below the age of 18 so long as they were tall and strong enough. The emperor agreed. But Wei Zheng refused to issue the imperial edict, though he was urged by the emperor several times. Then, beyond endurance, the emperor flew into a rage while Wei Zheng explained to him unhurriedly: "I once heard a story: in a distant village, people like to drain the lake to get more fish, but next year there would be no fish left. They prefer to burn the wood to catch beasts but next year there would be no beasts. If the men below 18 years old were all forced to join the army, how about the army recruitment in the future? Who are going to pay the state tax?" As to his suggestion, the emperor approved and gave another imperial edict claiming the men below 18 were excluded in the army recruitment.

Wei Zheng also gave advice to the emperor frequently on his personal life. Once the emperor visited Luoyang, he flew into a fury because the food prepared by the locals was not to his taste. Wei Zheng criticized the emperor directly: "Emperor Yang of Sui caused the demise of the state because of his excessive pursuit of pleasure and enjoyment. If you lose your temper just because the food served does not cater to your taste, how could ministers concentrate on the state affairs and keep honest and upright? Man's desire is endless. If things go on in this way, trouble and disaster will come up soon." The emperor felt astounded at his criticism: "If it were not you, I would never get a chance to hear these honest words." Since then, the emperor kept a frugal life all along.

Wei Zheng has worked for the emperor for 17 years, giving his advice frankly and directly to the emperor many times. Though his criticism seemed embarrassing and offensive, the emperor still regarded Wei Zheng as a loyal minister and trusted him with tolerance, magnanimity and appreciation. Because the emperor could take ministers' advice to correct his decisions and behaviors in time, his era, the "Reign of Zhenguan", was considered as a golden age that flourished economically and politically.

In the seventeenth year of Zhengguan Era (643 A.D.), Wei Zheng died. The emperor missed him greatly："Using copper mirror helps one to keep his dressing neat. Using history as a mirror helps one to see the cause of a state's rise and fall. Using a person as a mirror helps one to see the right and the wrong. When Wei Zheng died, I lost a mirror."

生难字/词注解 ｜ Notes

犯颜直谏：提一些让君王不开心但很中肯的意见或建议。
Admonish the emperor regardless of his face：Raise some advice that are useful but unpleasant to the ear that may offend the ruler.

谏：古代规劝君主或尊长，使其改正错误。
Give advice to the ruler：Give suggestions to emperors or the elders to advocate them to be aware of their errors in the ancient times.